One Little Chicken

by Elka Weber

Illustrations by Elisa Kleven

TRICYCLE PRESS

Berkeley

Oh, no!" screeched Mrs. Bendosa. "Where did that chicken come from? I just washed the floor!"

"I don't know." Leora pointed to the open gate. "Someone must have lost it. But can't we keep it? We could have fresh eggs for breakfast every day!"

The Bendosa family was poor—so poor, in fact, they rarely ate anything but lentil soup. And Leora was getting a little bored with lentil soup.

Mrs. Bendosa sighed. "You know the rule. Finders aren't keepers. This chicken isn't our chicken."

Mr. Bendosa came home just as the sun was setting. His back was hunched over from hard work, and he struggled along as though he carried the world on his shoulders.

Leora told him about the chicken.

"Your mother is right. We will just have to take care of the chicken until its owner returns. If I had a chicken of my own, I'd build it a coop."

Mr. Bendosa and Leora got to work with hammer and nails. Sawdust flew, wood shavings scattered, nails bent.

When they were through, they laid out a nice bed of straw.

“All this for a chicken we’re giving back? Now where will I plant my garden?” asked Mrs. Bendosa.

“Don’t worry, dear,” murmured Mr. Bendosa. “How much trouble is one little chicken?”

The very next morning, that chicken laid an egg. And then the next day, another. Every day for a week, Leora came home from school to find another egg.

"An omelet would be lovely," said Leora, looking at her bowl of lentil soup.

Mrs. Bendosa shook her head. "You know the rule. Finders aren't keepers. These eggs are not our eggs."

One day, the eggs began to hatch. Fuzzy yellow chicks filled the chicken coop. Then they got out of the coop and into the Bendosas' flowerpots . . .

under the pillows, on top of the books. Chicks were jumping everywhere.

"I can't get a moment's peace," grumbled Mrs. Bendosa.

So Leora and Mr. Bendosa gathered the hen and her chicks into a big basket and went to the market. They sold them all for two silver coins.

"What can we get for two silver coins?" Leora asked.

"We can buy a goat, one small goat," said Mr. Bendosa.

So Mr. Bendosa bought a small goat.

“A goat!” moaned Mrs. Bendosa. “I suppose you’re expecting me to milk it?”

“Just one goat,” said Mr. Bendosa. “How much trouble is one small goat?”

Every day, Leora and Mrs. Bendosa milked the goat. Then they separated the curds and whey to make cheese.

"Don't you just love cheesecake?" asked Leora.

"Yes," said Mrs. Bendosa. "But you know the rule—"

"Finders aren't keepers," Leora continued. "This cheese is not our cheese."

Mrs. Bendosa nodded.

The cheese didn't make noise or walk around the house, but if they kept it too long, it would start to smell funny. The cheese would have to go.

Leora and Mr. Bendosa took the cheese to the market. They sold it for two silver coins.

So they bought another small goat.

"Two goats?" wailed Mrs. Bendosa when they arrived home. "We barely have room for one!"

Mr. Bendosa shrugged. "It's easier than caring for a whole flock of chickens. How much trouble are two small goats?"

Before long, the two goats became a family of goats. There were goats everywhere—chewing the laundry, trampling the tiny vegetable patch, and eating the thatch right off the roof.

Mrs. Bendosa had had it. She stamped her feet and waved her arms. "I can't take it any longer. The noise! The smell! What a house!"

She ran out the gate and into the lane, followed by the goats.

Mrs. Bendosa bumped right into a man carrying a basket of chicks.

"What lovely goats you have," he said. "You don't happen to have a chicken, do you? A while back I was walking right around here and one of my chickens wandered off. I thought you might have seen her."

Mrs. Bendosa smiled for the first time in months.

Mr. Bendosa overheard the man and ran over to explain. "Oh! These aren't our goats at all. This herd of goats belongs to you, sir. You see. . . ."

And he told the stranger how one little chicken became many, many eggs and then more little chickens and then a small goat and then lots of cheese and then two small goats and then a whole herd of goats.

The man was amazed. “You did this all for me?”

“Well, of course,” said Leora. “We’re supposed to give back lost things. We just took care of your chicken until you came back.”

The man thanked them so much his mouth got tired.

Finally, the man went off with a basket of chickens in his arms and a whole herd of goats trailing behind him. He went straight to the market and sold all the chickens and goats for many, many silver coins. He used some of the money to buy vegetables and cheese for his family.

When the man returned home that night, he told his wife and son all about the Bendosas.

"Such wonderful people," said the wife, eating her supper.

The son did not hear the story. He was paying attention to something else. A little chicken had wandered into their yard, and it seemed to be lost.

I suppose we'll have to take care of it, he thought.

Oh, well, how much trouble is one little chicken?

Author's Note

One Little Chicken is the retelling of a story in the Talmud. Rabbi Chanina ben Dosa lived in Israel in the first century. He was so poor he sometimes had to live from one week to the next on nothing more than a few carob seeds, but he was so righteous that the Talmud says the entire world was sustained by his goodness.

Rabbi Chanina carefully followed all the teachings in the Torah. Among them is the directive to return lost property to its owner. ("If you see another person's animal, you shall not hide from it; you must return it to the owner. If the owner is not known to you, then you should bring the object into your house, where it shall remain until the owner inquires after it, and you will return it to him. So shall you do for his donkey, his garment, or any lost article that you may find. . . ." [Deut. 22:1–3])

One day a chicken wandered onto Rabbi Chanina's property. He took care of it and then invested the proceeds from the sale of the eggs and chicks in a herd of goats. When the owner came to reclaim his chicken, the rabbi gave him the entire herd of goats. Since the law would have allowed Rabbi Chanina to accept some payment for his troubles, returning the entire herd was an act of extreme piety.

Rabbi Chanina did have a daughter, but her name is not mentioned in the Talmud. I chose to call her Leora, because the Hebrew name means "I have light" and hints at a story elsewhere in the Talmud. Rabbi Chanina's daughter once mistakenly lit her Sabbath lamp with vinegar instead of oil. Although vinegar is not lamp fuel, the lamp burned and gave light for the entire Sabbath.

In *One Little Chicken*, Mrs. Bendosa comes off as something of a complainer. In fact, the Talmud praises Rabbi Chanina's wife for enduring her poverty with grace. Moreover, she was so holy that she regularly merited miracles being performed on her behalf. Saintliness on the order of Rabbi Chanina and his family may be beyond us, but we all have the power to enrich our lives with small acts of great kindness.

To my children and to sitting around the kitchen table. —E.W.

To Michael Oakleaf and his marvelous library.
And to Genelise Hazen, a lovely Leora. —E.K.

 Published in the United States by Tricycle Press, an imprint of Random House Children's Books, a division of Random House, Inc., New York.
www.randomhouse.com/kids

Library of Congress Cataloging-in-Publication Data
Weber, Elka, 1968-
One little chicken / by Elka Weber ; illustrations by Elisa Kleven. — 1st ed.
p. cm.
Summary: Retells a story in the Talmud about a family that cares for a lost chicken, turning its eggs into a profit which they later give to its owner.
[1. Lost and found possessions—Fiction. 2. Conduct of life—Fiction. 3. Chickens—Fiction. 4. Goats—Fiction. 5. Judaism—Customs and practices—Fiction.]
I. Kleven, Elisa, ill. II. Title.
PZ7.W3876One 2011
[E—dc22
2010008918

ISBN 978-1-58246-374-2 (hardcover)
ISBN 978-1-58246-401-5 (Gibraltar lib. bdg.)
ISBN 978-1-58246-458-9 (PJ Library)

Printed in Malaysia

Design by Chloe Rawlins
Typeset in P22 Kane and Aldine 721
The illustrations in this book were rendered in mixed-media collage with watercolors, ink, pastels, and colored pencils.

1 2 3 4 5 6 – 16 15 14 13 12 11

First Edition